Bear on the Train

For Patrick, the track that led to the bear — J.L.
For Alex, Eric and Lee — B.D.

Text copyright © 1999 by Julie Lawson
Illustrations copyright © 1999 by Brian Deines

Kids Can Press acknowledges the financial support of the Ontario Arts Council, the Canada
Council for the Arts and the Department of Cultural Heritage.

Published in Canada by
Kids Can Press Ltd.
29 Birch Avenue
Toronto, ON M4V 1E2

Published in the U.S. by
Kids Can Press Ltd.
85 River Rock Drive, Suite 202
Buffalo, NY 14207

The artwork in this book was rendered in oil on canvas.
Text is set in Bembo.

Edited by Debbie Rogosin
Designed by Marie Bartholomew

Printed in Hong Kong by Sheck Wah Tong Printing Press Limited

CM 99 0 9 8 7 6 5 4 3 2 1

Canadian Cataloguing in Publication Data

Lawson, Julie, 1947 –
        Bear on the train

ISBN 1-55074-560-3

I. Deines, Brian. II. Title.

PS8573.A94B42   1999   jC813'.54   C99-930239-6   PZ7.L38Be   1999

Kids Can Press is a Nelvana company.

Bear on the Train

Written by Julie Lawson

Illustrated by Brian Deines

Kids Can Press

One fall day, deep in the mountains, Bear smelled grain.

He followed the smell down the mountain, over the river, into a town, and onto a hopper of a westbound train.

Nobody saw him but Jeffrey.

"Hey, Bear!" Jeffrey shouted. "Get off the train!"

Bear paid no attention.

He plunked himself down on the platform and began to eat the grain.

He ate and ate till his belly was bursting.

Then he gave a long, rumbly belch of contentment.

Nobody heard him but Jeffrey.

Slowly the train began to roll.

Jeffrey ran alongside the tracks shouting,

"Hey, Bear! Get off the train!
You'll freeze when it snows and get wet when it rains!
You'll be scared in the tunnels; you'll be all alone!
Your friends will be worried; they'll want you back home!
So, Bear! Get off the train!"

Bear paid no attention.

He crawled inside the hopper, shuffled a bit, and
lay down. Then he yawned and closed his eyes.

The train rolled faster.

It plunged into dark, spiraling tunnels.

It swayed over high trestle bridges.

Bear didn't care.

Bear wasn't scared.

Bear was sound asleep.

The train whistled at the crossings.

It roared down the canyon and thundered through the woods.

It hugged the towering cliffs that rose above the river.

And all the while, Bear snored and snuffled and dreamed of grain — hoppers and hills and mountains of grain.

The train rolled through a day and through a night.

When it reached the coast, the grain was unloaded, one hopper car at a time.

Bear gave a loud snort as the hatches on his car were opened.

Out poured the grain, and the hatches were closed.

Bear stirred as the train lurched forward.

But nobody noticed.

And soon the train was on its way, heading east to the prairie for more grain.

Through a night and through a day the train rolled on — through the woods and up the canyon, over high trestle bridges, in and out of spiraling tunnels — until it reached the little town.

Bear snuzzled and snorted and dreamed.

Nobody saw him but Jeffrey.

Jeffrey waved and yelled,

"Hey, Bear! Get off the train!
You'll freeze when it snows and get wet when it rains!
You'll be scared in the tunnels; you'll be all alone!
Your friends will be worried; they'll want you back home!
So, Bear! Get off the train!"

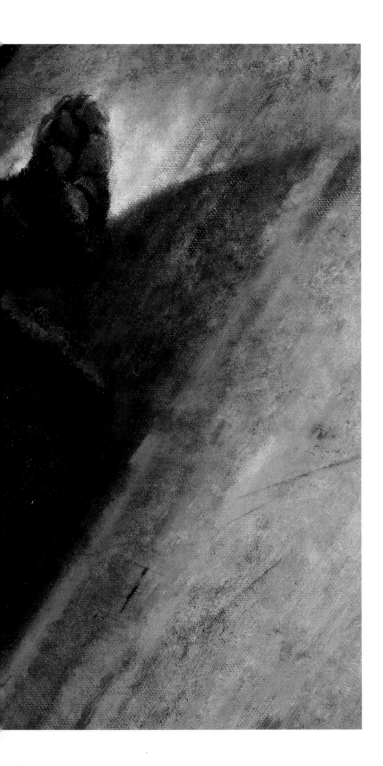

Bear paid no attention.

He slept as the train rocked and rolled out of town.

He slept through the mountains.

He slept through the foothills.

He slept across the prairie.

He slept all the way to a siding.

And there the train stopped.

One by one the empty hopper cars were loaded with more grain.

Bear licked his lips. He scratched his belly.

Then he yawned and kept on dreaming.

Nobody noticed.

The train rolled away to the west.

Leaves shivered and fell in the wind.

Icicles gleamed and glittered.

Geese flew over the grassland.

Bear slept on, as snow began to fall.

Once again the train pulled into the little town.

Bear crawled sleepily onto the platform. He raised his head,
gave a few half-hearted sniffs, then crawled back inside
the hopper.

Nobody saw him but Jeffrey.

He jumped up and down and hollered,

"Hey, Bear! Get off the train!
You'll freeze when it snows and get wet when it rains!
You'll be scared in the tunnels; you'll be all alone!
Your friends will be worried; they'll want you back home!
So, Bear! Get off the train!"

Bear paid no attention.

He slept through the rumble of wheels on rails, the squeal of brakes and the clamor of crews.

He slept through to the coast and back to the prairie.

He slept to the east and he slept to the west, through weeks of snow and months of cold, dreaming of bright yellow grain.

Little by little, the ice began to melt.

Snow turned to rain.

Blossoms fell in the wind.

Geese flew over the grassland.

One day as the train pulled into the little town, Bear smelled something different.

He opened his eyes and growled a low, waking-up growl.

He stretched his legs and sniffed the morning air.

Then he lumbered down from the hopper.

Jeffrey saw him and cheered.

"Yeaaay, Bear! You got off the train!
You rode through the snow and the wind and the rain.
Now you won't be afraid and you won't be alone.
Your friends will be happy to see you back home.
Yeaaay, Bear! You got off the train!"

Bear paid no attention.

He twitched his nose and sniffed again.

Then he followed the smell away from the train, out of the town, over the river … to the succulent taste of spring.

He ate and ate and ate — along the riverbank, up the grassy slope, and into the new-green growth of the mountainside.

And nobody saw him but Jeffrey.